We hope the words and images in this story
foster transformative conversations that lead to change.

That
FLAG

written by **Tameka Fryer Brown**

illustrated by **Nikkolas Smith**

HARPER
An Imprint of HarperCollinsPublishers

Bianca and I are almost twins. We're the same in so many ways.

We both wear our hair in braids.
We spend independent reading time together.

We play four square better than anyone in our class.

We're inseparable. She's my best friend.

But only at school. I'm not allowed to go to her house, even though we live on the same street.

"Keira," Mom says whenever I go outside. "Please stay where I can see you."

Then she shoots a look that means, *Don't go anywhere near their yard.*

I know why. It's because of that flag.

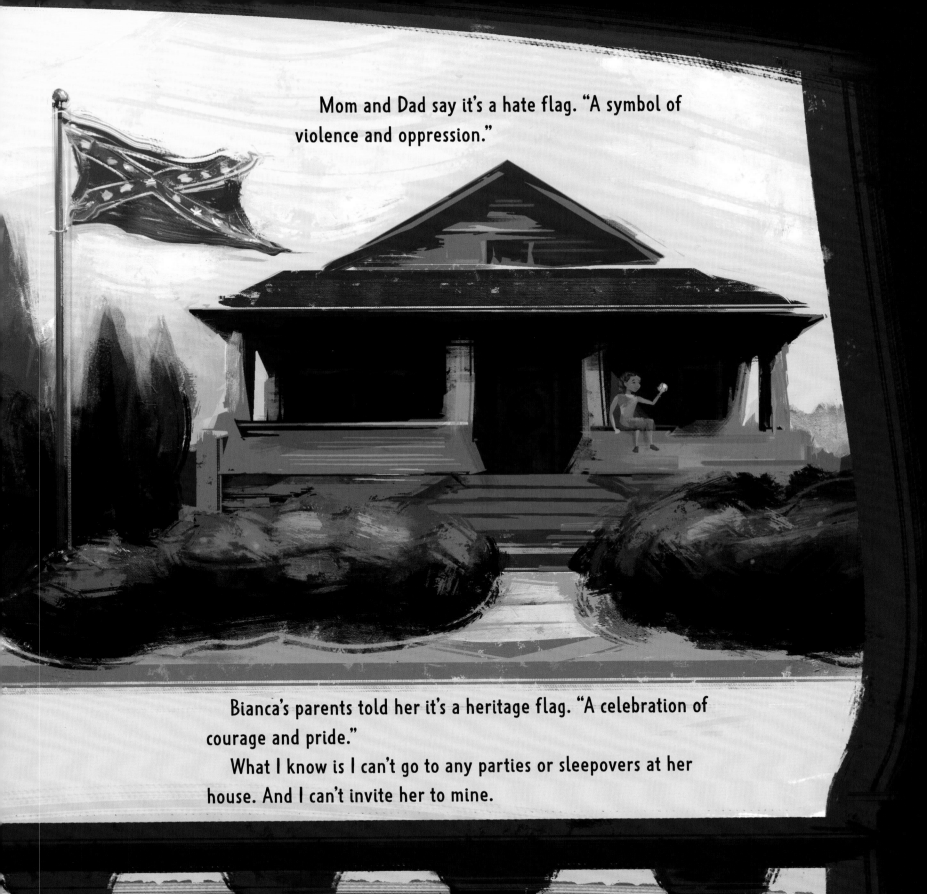

Mom and Dad say it's a hate flag. "A symbol of violence and oppression."

Bianca's parents told her it's a heritage flag. "A celebration of courage and pride."

What I know is I can't go to any parties or sleepovers at her house. And I can't invite her to mine.

At bedtime, before my parents tuck me in, I remember my field trip form.

"It's for the Southern Legacy Museum," Dad says. "They have a new exhibit. Mind if I tag along?"

I don't mind. Dad is a lot of fun. He even buys me souvenirs sometimes. "Sure," I say.

Mom and Dad hug me tight. For an extra-long time.

On field trip day, once we're off the bus, Bianca
and I link hands.
We wait for Ms. Greyson to call our names.
Oh no! She's assigned us to different groups!

When I start to frown, Dad tugs my braids, makes a face, and smiles.
I can't help but smile back. I'm glad Dad's here with me.

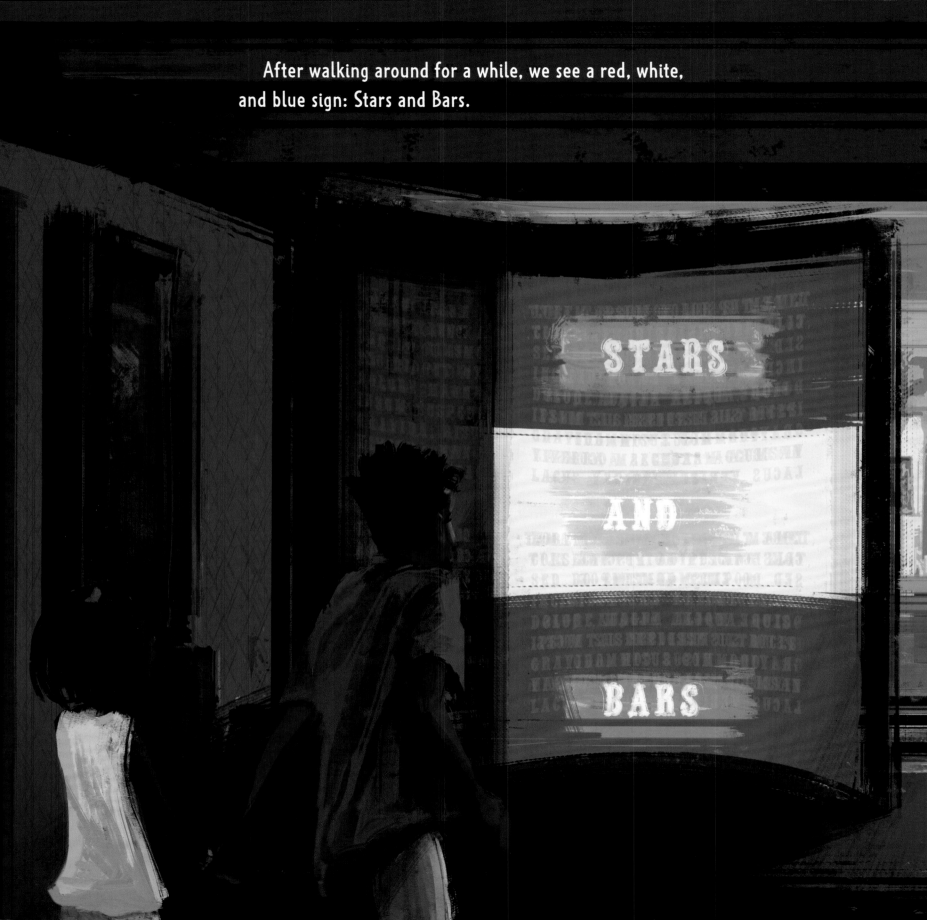

After walking around for a while, we see a red, white, and blue sign: Stars and Bars.

Dad takes my hand. "This is something we need to see."

First, we see a frilly dress from antebellum days.

I picture myself wearing it and giggle. I'd look pretty silly.

There's a cotton gin with lots of little
puffy plants around it.
"Wish we could pick some off," I say.
Dad glances but doesn't say anything.

When we come to an auction block, Dad freezes.
He's not smiling at all.
Neither am I.

In silence, Dad and I walk to a glass case filled with old
photographs.
I see soda fountains, poodle skirts, gigantic cars with fins . . .
dogs and water hoses . . .
teenagers crying in the streets . . .
scary men in white gowns holding torches and flags.

That flag.

"*Keira!*"

Bianca runs up to me. "I've been looking for you everywhere!"

She throws her arms around my neck, but I don't hug her back.

"What's wrong?" she asks.

My throat feels tight. I'm not sure what to say.

I just point to the pictures in the case, then I walk away.

Back on the bus, Dad and I sit up front, behind the driver.
I stare out the window, remembering those pictures and that flag.
My best friend's flag.

Later that night, my family and I talk for a long time. They tell me
things they've never told me about before.

About the scary things my grandpa saw when he was just a kid.

About Grandma being spat on for trying to go to school.

About Mom and Dad getting called bad names and chased by people in a truck.

About the Freedom Riders.

About Selma.

About the Charleston 9.

We talk about the things Black people have to do every day to stay safe.
After our talk, I feel scared, confused, and mad.
But mostly I'm sad.

At school the next day, I wait for Bianca to say
something about the pictures.
She talks about her puppy instead.

I guess those pictures didn't bother her.
I guess we're not the same.
I guess we're not best friends after all.

During reading time, I read by myself.

At recess, I jump rope alone.

When Ms. Greyson asks what we learned from our field trip, I say,
"The Confederate flag is racist."

"That's not true!" Bianca cries. "It stands for Southern pride."

"The Confederacy," Ms. Greyson says, "fought a war to keep Black people enslaved.
Their battle flag is still used by hate groups who want white people to rule."

"No." Bianca shakes her head. "Why would my family fly a flag like that?"

"I don't know," Ms. Greyson answers, "but it's a good question to ask."

I'm trying to beat my grandpa at chess when I hear Grandma cry,
"Lord have mercy!"
Mom turns up the news. It's news none of us wants to hear.

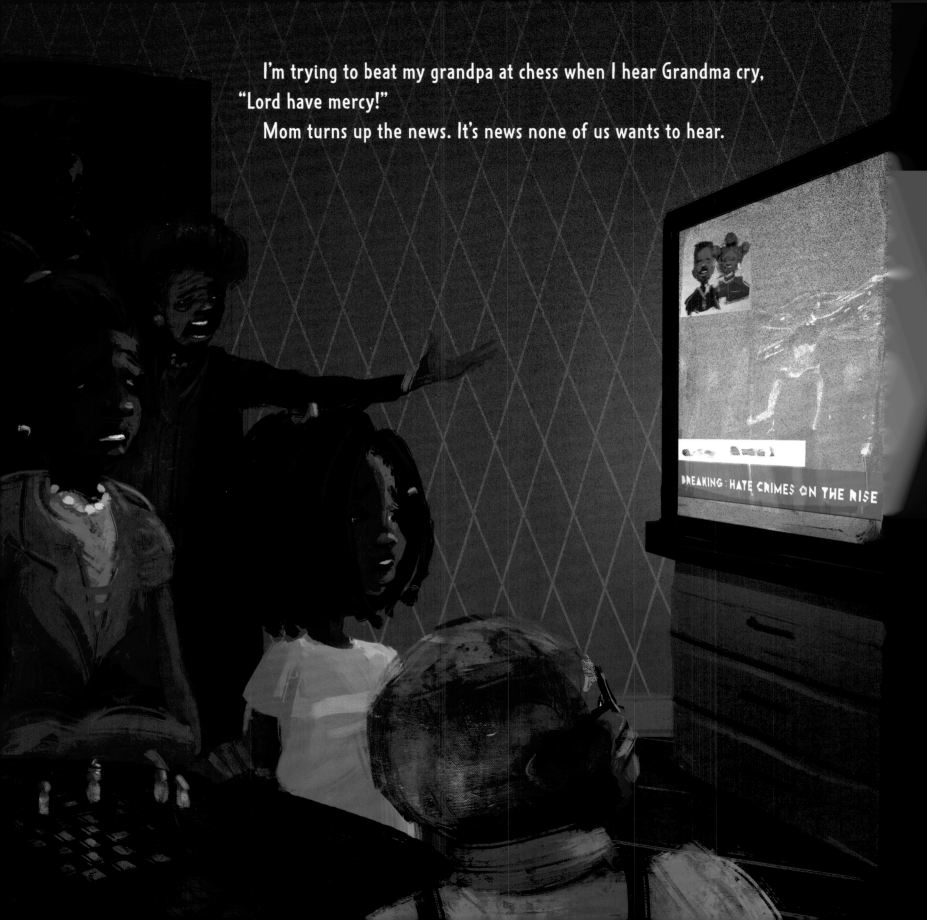

Two Black people were shot in their own front yard by three white men.
They show pictures of the men on TV. They're standing in front of that flag.

That hate flag.

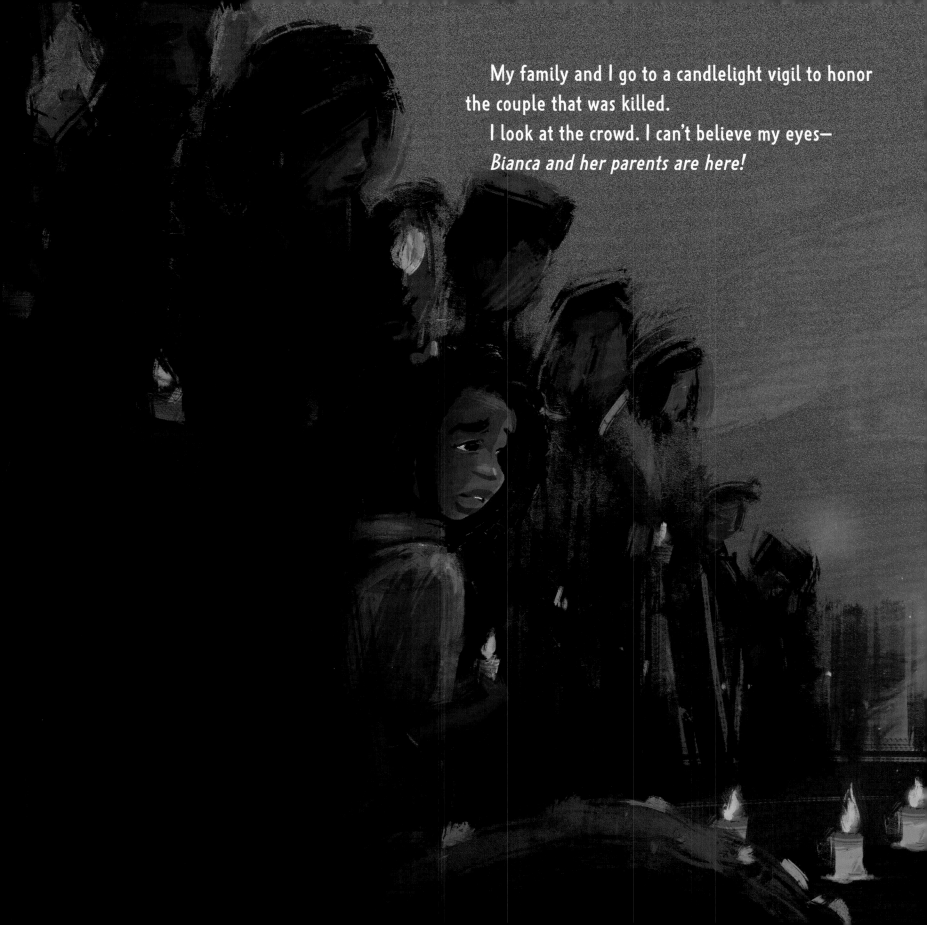

My family and I go to a candlelight vigil to honor the couple that was killed.
I look at the crowd. I can't believe my eyes—
Bianca and her parents are here!

I did not expect her family to come.
I wonder why they did.

Coming home, we see a new house flying that flag.
It makes my heart hurt, so I look away.

We pass Bianca's house. *They've taken theirs down!*
I can't stop staring.
I wonder why they did.

As the late bell rings the next morning at
school, Bianca passes me a note:
    "You were right."

I haven't spoken to Bianca for days. No sharing
books or playing four square at recess.
But now, that flag is gone from her house . . .
so maybe things can be different.
Maybe we can be friends after all.
I don't know.

But I'm willing to see.

ABOUT THE CONFEDERATE FLAG

From 1860 to 1861, eleven states seceded (or broke away) from the United States of America in an act of insurrection. They called themselves the Confederate States of America, or the Confederacy. On April 12, 1861, the Confederacy started the Civil War by attacking Fort Sumter. They went to war to protect their ability to hold Black people captive in a system known as slavery—a system through which they had accumulated great wealth. They also did not consider Black people to be equal to white people and did not care about Black people's right to exist as free human beings. The Confederacy fought to maintain this violent and oppressive system of slavery at all costs.

The Confederacy began flying its first official flag, the Stars and Bars, in March 1861. The Stars and Bars, however, looked too much like the American flag and caused confusion for the Confederate soldiers on the battlefield. They adopted a battle flag late that year, an early version of what most call the Confederate flag today. It is also known as the Rebel flag and the Dixie flag.

Activist Bree Newsome removes the Confederate flag from the South Carolina State House in protest after a white supremacist killed nine Black people at Emanuel AME Church in Charleston, SC, during evening Bible study. (Reuters/ Adam Anderson)

While the Confederacy ultimately lost the Civil War in 1865, their battle flag has remained a symbol for hate groups throughout the years and to this very day. From the Ku Klux Klan, who carried it during the 1950s and '60s as they fought to stop integration and the civil rights movement . . . to the white nationalists who marched with it in 2017 in opposition to the removal of Confederate monuments from public spaces in Charlottesville, Virginia, . . . to the insurrectionists who brought it inside the US Capitol building on January 6, 2021, for the first time in our nation's history, as a violent mob sought to prevent the president-elect from taking office.

Despite all these facts, there are still those who say the Confederate flag simply stands for Southern heritage and Southern pride. However, the Confederate flag cannot magically be separated from its racist origins nor from its continued association with white supremacy. It is only by acknowledging the entire truth of our history—including the unflattering parts—that we will finally be able to overcome the racism embedded in our society. We must never be afraid to ask questions and seek out truth, for it is the truth that will set us all free.

AUTHOR'S NOTE

I wrote this story to tell you the truth about the Confederate flag, about where it came from and how it has been used throughout our country's history. I want to help readers understand why it is not merely a symbol of "Southern heritage," but an emblem that makes many people feel anger and fear—and for good reason. I believe in telling kids the truth, even about things that are sad or a little bit scary.

I'm not sure when I was first told to stay away from people who flew or wore the Confederate flag . . . but I'm sure it was

by someone who loved me and cared about my safety. What they didn't tell me was why those people could be a danger to me, and that left me confused. It wasn't until I was an adult that I learned just how often the Confederate flag has been used by white supremacists in our country. White supremacists believe white people are better than Black people and other groups, and they believe white people should control our society. I wrote this book because I believe white supremacy is wrong, and that celebrating the symbols associated with it (like Confederate flags and statues) is wrong too.

If human beings can learn to be racist, we can also learn not to be. In fact, your generation could grow up to be the fairest, most inclusive generation our nation has ever seen . . . especially if we adults do our part and tell you more truths about more things.

I wrote *That Flag* to do my part to make humanity better, because I believe in your power to change the world.

ILLUSTRATOR'S NOTE

I truly believe that America is a country that can soar to the highest heights if we are open and honest about our past.

In *That Flag*, I wanted to illustrate the feelings of hurt and sadness that come with the past and present of the Confederate flag, and toward the end of the book, paint visual representations of what society could look like if we are truly serious about addressing and confronting the monster that is racism. It is a monster that I have seen firsthand as a young Black boy growing up in the South, but I also grew up seeing many people who believe in a free and equitable society. This has led me to creating artivism for a living, with the primary objective of illustrating both the hurt and the hope in this world.

I love to portray the innocence and wisdom of youth because it is often a roadmap of where we should go as a human race, and Keira and Bianca display this so well. To all of you youngsters out there who stand up and speak out for human rights and justice for all, thank you for leading the way to a brighter future. Never let anyone silence your voice.

SOURCE NOTES AND RECOMMENDED READING

Blakermore, Erin. "How the Confederate Battle Flag Became an Enduring Symbol of Racism." *National Geographic*, January 12, 2021, www.nationalgeographic.com/history/article/how-confederate-battle-flag-became-symbol-racism.

"Taking Down the Confederate Flag." Facing History & Ourselves, www.facinghistory.org/resource-library/taking-down-confederate-flag. (Connection questions included.)

"(1861) Alexander H. Stephens, 'Cornerstone Speech.'" BlackPast, November 27, 2012, www.blackpast.org/african-american-history/1861 -alexander-h-stephens-cornerstone-speech.

"The Declaration of Causes of Seceding States (Primary Sources)." American Battlefield Trust, www.battlefields.org/learn/primary-sources /declaration-causes-seceding-states.

"The Lost Cause: Definition and Origins." American Battlefield Trust, October 30, 2020, www.battlefields.org/learn/articles/lost-cause -definition-and-origins.

For you, dear reader. Never be afraid of
the truth. It makes us better people.
—T.F.B.

To every human being standing
for justice in the face of injustice.
—N.S.

That Flag
Text copyright © 2023 by Tameka Fryer Brown
Illustrations copyright © 2023 by Nikkolas Smith
All rights reserved. Manufactured in Italy.
No part of this book may be used or reproduced in any manner whatsoever
without written permission except in the case of brief quotations embodied in critical
articles and reviews. For information address HarperCollins Children's Books,
a division of HarperCollins Publishers, 195 Broadway, New York, NY 10007.
www.harpercollinschildrens.com

Library of Congress Control Number: 2022930129
ISBN 978-0-06-309344-7

The artist used Photoshop to create the digital illustrations for this book.
Typography by Rachel Zegar
22 23 24 25 26   RTLO   10 9 8 7 6 5 4 3 2 1
❖
First Edition